We Love Halloween!

Based on the original teleplay by Eric Weiner
Cover illustrated by Jason Fruchter
Interior illustrated by Susan Hall

A GOLDEN BOOK • NEW YORK

ISBN: 978-0-375-86513-8
www.randomhouse.com/kids
Printed in the United States of America
10 9 8 7 6 5

¡Hola! I'm getting ready for Halloween!

¡Hola! I'm getting ready for Halloween!

Which costumes should Boots and I wear?

Maybe I can be a pirate!

And Boots can be my first mate!

Or maybe I'll be a princess!

And Boots can be a prince!

Will you draw lines to match Boots's costumes to their spooky shadows?

I know! I'll wear my cat costume!

"Happy Halloween, Dora! Can you guess my costume?"

"I'm a fire chicken! I couldn't decide between a chicken and a firefighter. So I'm both! *Bawk! Bawk!*"

Will you draw yourself in costume?

Whoa! You surprised us, Little Monster!

"Dora, when the little arrow on the Big Clock gets to the 12, all monsters must be home! But I'm lost."

What time is it now? Help Little Monster find out by looking at the number that the little hand is pointing to. Then draw that many circles below the clock.

It's 9:00! We'd better check Map to find out
how to get to Little Monster's house.

Map says we have to go through the Pumpkin Patch and the Good Witch's Forest to get to Little Monster's house.

Will you help us find the Pumpkin Patch?
Trace the path that leads to it.

Look at all the silly bats! How many do you see?

Help Dora's friends find their Halloween costumes by following the lines!

Hey! We can trick-or-treat on the way
to Little Monster's house.

Will you decorate this trick-or-treat basket?

Treats! Hooray! Thank you! ¡Gracias!

There's our friend Scarecrow in the Pumpkin Patch.
He can help us get Little Monster home.

To get through the Patch, the scarecrow says to find the pumpkins that match.

Will you help me find the jack-o'-lantern that matches mine?

Will you use your crayons and stickers to turn this pumpkin into a jack-o'-lantern?

It's getting late! Will you draw an arrow pointing to the 10 on the Big Clock?

Now we have to find the Good Witch's Forest. But look! It's Abuela's house. Can you guess what her costume will be? Connect the dots for a hint.

I see more trick-or-treaters! What is Diego dressed as? What is Big Red Chicken dressed as?

Can you find the real Diego?
(Hint: He's the one who looks different.)

Did you hear that? It sounds like Swiper!
That sneaky fox will try to swipe our candy.
Do you see Swiper?

Swiper, no swiping!

Swiper, if you want some candy, just say
"Trick or treat!"

Will you draw the picture
that completes each pattern?

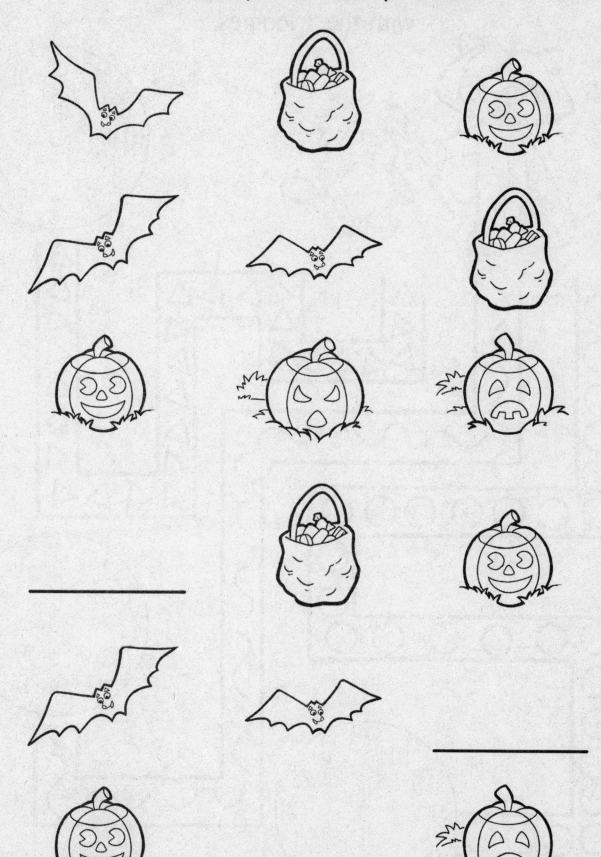

It's the Big Clock! Help Dora and Little Monster find out what time it is by following the path with the triangles.

We made it! The Good Witch's Forest is on the other side of the gate! To open the gate, say "Abre."

The Good Witch is giving us her broomstick so we can fly quickly through the Forest.

Yay, look! ¡Estrellas! Help us catch the stars by using the chart to color them.

1=Yellow
2=Blue
3=Red
4=Orange
5=Green

We're almost to Little Monster's house!
But we'd better hurry.
Which path will get us there the quickest?

It's 12 o'clock! We brought Little Monster home
just in time for. . .the Halloween Party!
And we're invited, too!

We did it! Thanks for helping! Happy Halloween!

Decorate your treat bag!

- Color the pictures.
- Ask a grown-up to cut them out.
- Tape the pictures onto your bag!

HAPPY HALLOWEEN!